A Slice of Honeybear Pie

By Eva Wilder & Jacqueline Sweet

Chapter 1
Bearly Escaped

"Ma'am, you are in a heap of trouble."

The officer leaning over the car was bleary-eyed and resembled nothing so much as a wrinkly faced mutt stuffed into a uniform. His short collar was buttoned too tight around his neck and folds of flesh hung over on all sides. At least he had kind eyes.

Mina tried to focus on his badge, to read what it said, but her eyes couldn't resolve the words. They seemed to be upside down. She blinked and tears rolled up her forehead. She was crying she noticed.

Also she seemed to be upside down.

"You mind telling me what happened?" The officer stooped down. He was peering at Mina through the window of her car, but the angle was all wrong.

Suddenly it came to her.

"I flipped my car," she said, her voice making clear she'd only just realized it.

"Yeah," the cop said with a drawl. "I sorta figured that part out. We have a wrecker on the way to tow it up out of here."

"Where am I?" She wanted to ask how long she'd been out, how far she'd made it outside of San Francisco before her accident. If she'd gotten as far as Oregon, maybe she'd be safe.

"You're in Bearfield, about two hours north-ish of the city." The cop's face came into focus. It was possible Mina had a concussion. She remembered the crash hazily, as if it was a dream that evaporated upon waking. She'd been fleeing the city. The whole business deal had collapsed. She was broke, sure, but also with what she now knew about her business partners she was also in terrible danger.

She recalled gas station coffee. A packet of those foul yellow pills her sister called Trucker Speed that gave her jittery nerves and a sour taste on her tongue that didn't even keep her awake as she drove. There'd been winding mountain roads with a suggested speed limit of 30. She'd been doing nearly twice that.

She was lucky she wasn't dead.

"What's your name, ma'am?" The cop was wearing slippers, she noticed. They were red flannel and worn around the toes. In a flash she knew she could trust this bumpkin sheriff with her life, but that he'd be no match for the men who were after her. He'd do the right thing, sure, and file an accident report and contact her emergency numbers and a file would be made in his system.

A Slice of Honeybear Pie

And the men who were after her would see that file and know where she was. And she wouldn't live another night.

"I need a lawyer," she said. Nothing seemed to be broken. Her chest hurt like hell where the belt had caught her, but she was otherwise unharmed as far as she could tell. But what did she know? She was a baker, not a doctor.

"There's no crime as far as I can see. I just need to file a report and have you blow a breathalyzer, but it's just a formality. Unless of course you decide to be belligerent and I really wish you wouldn't. It's four in the morning and my shift doesn't technically start until eight. I'd much rather be at home keeping my wife warm."

"I can't give you my name," Mina said. "And I won't give you a fake name. That'd be a crime."

"I need a name for my report, girl. So either you give me yours right now, or I arrest you for unsafe driving and obstruction of justice and resisting arrest and a few other things that I'm sure I'll think of on the way to the station." He kicked some of the car wreckage farther down the mountain where it bounced off a tree with a thunk. "Littering, maybe."

It sucked that she had to inconvenience this poor guy. He was just trying to do his job. But if he did it by the book, they'd find her.

"I'm sorry about this, but as far as you're concerned my name is *get me a lawyer.*"

# # #

Matt Morrissey didn't want to answer the phone. Good news never came at five in the morning. Well, except birth announcements. But since he'd never gotten anyone pregnant and his brothers—as far as Matt knew—had never knocked up any of their tourist hook-ups, it seemed unlikely. But it was the work phone. You don't get to ignore the work phone.

There wasn't a lot of work for a backwoods attorney, so whatever came his way he had to jump on it. If he didn't, Arnold Pimsler would. And no one deserved representation by Arnold Pimsler, no matter how guilty they might be.

The bear in Matt wanted to sleep until noon. It wanted pancakes and three cups of coffee with plenty of milk and sugar before it even considered having contact with normal humans. If the bear was in charge though, Matt never would have made it through high school, let alone law school.

"Pete," he said. "You got something for me?" Matt fought to keep the growl out of his voice.

"How'd you know it was me?"

Matt sighed. Why couldn't he just be asleep? "Caller ID, Sheriff. What's up?"

"Oh right," the old sheriff chuckled. "Well, anyway, we got a wreck up here on Strawberry Road and the lady involved is asking for a lawyer."

"You charged her?" Pete never charged anyone he didn't have to, especially not women.

"She really forced my hand on this one. I tellya, she's either guilty of something awful or running from something twice as bad."

Mysterious women wrecking their cars sounded like a lot of billable hours to the man in Matt, but to the bear it sounded like a whole lot of work.

A Slice of Honeybear Pie

"Get Jolene to put on a fresh pot, willya?" Matt grumbled. "I'll be there as soon as I can."

"Hey Matt," Pete said, just as he was about to hang up.

"Yeah?"

"Dress nice for this one, kid." There was a knowing tone in Pete's voice that Matt didn't like.

Life in Bearfield was never a particularly formal affair. The town was too small and too sleepy for anyone to get too bothered about anything. They were just far enough away from San Francisco and Sacramento and Napa to get the weekend tourist trade, but also to be completely ignored by most of the world. With a population hovering somewhere around four thousand souls, spread out over twenty-five sprawling miles of forest and mountain and stream, Bearfield was a quiet place to live. Matt wore suits to court when he had to—

but only because the local court was run by the

neighboring town of Poppy Valley. If the court had been

in Bearfield, the judge would have shown up an hour late

for everything, dressed in a flannel shirt over yoga pants.

It was just that kind of place. Foggy in the morning,

sunny in the afternoon, and with a night sky so full of

stars that it felt like you could jump off the mountain

and catch them—Matt loved Bearfield with every inch of

his skin. His family had been settled there longer than

the place had a name.

Driving in to the police station, the curving mountain

roads were empty. Later in the day there'd be delivery

trucks bringing fresh food to the Lodge and to the

quaint bed-and-breakfasts nestled in the bosom of the

mountains. Then there'd be the tourists flooding the

roads as they sought out hiking trails and wineries and

cool clear brooks to swim in. Matt knew the rhythms of

A Slice of Honeybear Pie

Bearfield like he knew the the sound of the breath in his lungs. He knew everyone who lived in the town and many of the regular tourists as well. They all agreed it was a magical place to live or to visit. They had no idea just how magical it was.

Matt pulled his battered Jeep into the police station parking lot alongside Pete's cruiser and Jolene's sporty little coupe. The sun still hadn't risen yet and the morning fog hung on the tree tops thick and white. His bear rolled over and grumped. Matt should have been asleep, but he had a job to do and so he was doing it to the best of his ability. The station had the classic look of an early seventies A-frame repurposed into a civic building, because that's what it was. When the town decided ages ago they needed an actual police force (aka, Pete) to deal with speeders and the occasional Lodge guest who got a bit too ripped on local wine, they took an empty house and converted it into the station. It was cozy, like everything else in Bearfield, but also a little odd.

The master bedroom of the A-frame was Pete's office and the living room was Jolene's. The sassy woman was Matt's distant cousin, like half of Bearfield, and she ran the 911 board, the police station, and half of city hall out of the little house. The second bedroom was the holding room and jail cell, though it still had the ornamental rug and off-white walls of the pre-police station home. They never really needed to hold anyone and so hadn't bothered putting in bars or even a door that locked.

"Matthew," Jolene said, peering at him over her cat's eye glasses as he entered the station. "Fresh pot on for ya. Got some leftover crullers from the Lodge, too."

"No bear claws?" Matt joked as he took two of the stale donuts. Jolene was one of the few people in town who knew his secret.

Jolene rose from her desk with a serious expression and walked over to Matt. She was half his size and twice his age. "I thought Pete told you to dress nice?"

"Hey, this is my second best suit."

Jolene sighed in exasperation and shook her head. She buttoned Matt's jacket and stepped back, examining him.

"What's going on with you two?" Matt asked.

"Straighten your tie."

"Yes, ma'am," Matt grinned.

"Would it kill ya to shave before seeing a client?"

"Pete said to hurry."

"And shaving takes an hour?"

Matt shrugged. He thought he looked good with a little stubble.

"If your daddy could see you now." Jolene's wrinkled expression implied that he'd be less than impressed.

Matt wished his father had been able to express his disappointment, but the man had been hibernating for ten years now, stuck in bear form after a vicious hunter attack. He slumbered deep in the mountains, in a cave that stretched for miles underground, next to dozens of other werebears that were probably Matt's extended kin. Matt and his brothers had carried his dad down there, sweating and straining under the weight of the big animal. They said that you couldn't kill a werebear, that they were immortal. But do enough damage and the big men just went to sleep as their bodies and minds knit themselves back together. Every few decades one of the old bears woke up and had to be reintroduced to modern society. Matt's dad could wake up tomorrow or in twenty years. There was no way to tell.

Matt didn't like thinking about it.

"She give a name yet?" Matt asked, nodding at the interrogation room.

"She says her name is get me a lawyer." Jolene pursed her lips in annoyance. "City girls."

"Well, if I find out I'll let you know, 'kay?" Matt stuffed one whole donut in his mouth and washed it down with an entire cup of coffee. The bear wasn't remotely satisfied, but it was a start. He'd have to swing by the Lodge after the client meeting to get the biggest spread he could find, otherwise the bear would be grumbling all day, putting Matt in a sour mood. He wiped the crumbs off his face and poured another coffee and one more for the client then backed into the room, using his butt to push the door open.

He turned, and nearly dropped both cups. Sitting at the table, with her hands folded politely in front of her, was the most beautiful woman he'd ever seen. She had warm brown skin like sunset shadows on the face of the mountain, and soft curly hair that framed her face perfectly. She wore a leather jacket over a red cotton dress that outlined her ample curves. Matt wanted to bend over and look under the table to see what kind of shoes she was wearing but he decided that'd be inappropriate. He was so used to the sporty, tanned, skinny tourist girls with their spandex or lycra or whatever leaving nothing to the imagination. Those kinds of women may have driven his brothers crazy, but they did nothing at all for him. Matt craved soft curves he could bury himself in, a woman with substance. And here she was.

A Slice of Honeybear Pie

His bear stopped grumping and sat up inside him and then roared. *This one*, it said. *This one is your mate.*

Chapter 2
Bearly Legal

Mina could not believe the police station. It was just someone's home, with the furniture removed. There was no security. Hell, she didn't even see a gun in the place. How could these people protect her? What use would they be if Harker came around?

The holding room was tidy at least, even if was just a rustic bedroom with a desk in the middle. The old cop, Pete, hadn't even bothered handcuffing her. Mina was fairly certain she could have walked out whenever she wanted without him stopping her. But then what? She'd wrecked her car. It was a miracle she wasn't more hurt from the accident. Aside from the bruising in her chest where the seat belt had caught her and a bump on her head, she was fine. But with no car and no money and the evidence she had on Harker still in the glove compartment, she was thoroughly screwed.

Could she open up to the old cop? He seemed nice enough. But the last thing Mina wanted was to drag anyone else into her mess. The last person she'd gone to for help was already dead.

Just as she was about to give in to despair, the door opened and *he* walked in.

Dressed in a rumpled brown suit with a matching necktie cinched too tight around his neck, the man wasn't dressed well, but it didn't matter. He was so big he had to duck to clear the doorway and so wide that he had to turn sideways to fit. He was muscular and lean and massive and looked like he was built on a different scale than the rest of the world. And he was gorgeous, with wavy brown hair, deep brown eyes and a face that belonged in a museum, with a strong nose and high cheekbones and a square jaw dusted with stubble.

Mina took one look at him and lost her breath. Men didn't really look like him. Or at least, not outside of the movies they didn't. She wondered what he looked like naked and then immediately felt embarrassed. There was too much at stake to get swept away by a pretty face and a perfect body. Closing her eyes, she forced herself to breathe. She thought about Harker and his beautiful blue eyes, the way he kissed her, the sight of him holding a smoking gun. You couldn't trust a pretty man. You couldn't trust your heart. The fire inside would warm you, it would drive you crazy, but it'd burn you up as well.

The big man sat down across from her, the chair groaning under his weight. He smelled like pine trees and sugar with a hint of animal musk that made her knees so weak she glad she was already seated.

"I'm Matt," he said, his voice clear and calm like a mountain stream. "What should I call you?"

"You're my attorney?"

"I am. So anything you have to say is protected. Attorney-client privilege."

"You don't look like a lawyer," she said, trying to keep her voice neutral but the lust she felt was there, a swift undercurrent.

"With this suit? Who else would wear this?" He flashed a relaxed and boyish grin at her. And inexplicably, Mina felt like everything would work out. If you looked up reassuring in the dictionary there'd be a picture of this guy's smile. He produced a yellow legal pad from a battered satchel and clicked a pen to life. "Tell me what you're running from, maybe I can help."

Mina liked the way he's eyes sparked when he said *help*. She liked it a lot.

No, she couldn't do this. Begone hormones! She was a grown-ass woman. She'd opened her own business. She wasn't some fifteen-year-old to get swept away by a pretty face.

"I can't tell you my name. I can't be in the system. There are men looking for me. Dangerous men."

# # #

Matt leaned back in his chair and tossed the pen onto the pad. "Tell me about these men." The thought of anyone threatening this beautiful woman made his man and his bear both very angry. The world was tough enough by itself, it didn't need evil men preying upon innocent, curvy, voluptuous, cocoa-skinned women with lips that were made for kissing.

"You're a big guy. You live out here in the forest or whatever so I'm sure you think you're tough. But you don't know the men who are after me. You don't want to know them." The woman's voice shook with fear as she spoke. She was trying to hold it together and failing. She was strong—she'd have to be to get through a car accident and not end up a sobbing mess—but there were limits to strength.

Unless you were Matt.

Matt took off his suit coat, it was always too warm in the station, especially for him. Being a shifter meant his blood ran hot anyway. He unbuttoned his shirt cuffs and rolled up his sleeves, revealing his thickly corded forearms as large as saplings.

"Please trust me when I tell you I can take care of myself," he said, putting a hint of a growl into his voice. If he didn't know it would drive her stark raving mad with terror, he would have shifted right there to show her. Well, maybe outside. He was pretty big as a bear and he'd hate to smash up anymore furniture.

"Can you get me out of here? The men who are after me, they want me gone. They're undoubtedly searching every inch of Northern California for me right now." Her eyes were wide, her breathing shallow. Matt's enhanced shifter senses could hear her heart hammering in her chest. He could smell the sour tang of fear wafting off her, mixed with the sugary head-spinning scent of lust. She wanted him. He knew it.

"Did you bring your cell phone?"

"Of course, it's right here." The woman slid the phone across the table. Matt picked it up and shattered it in his hand with one quick squeeze, letting the glass and plastic and printed circuits rain to the table with a clatter.

"If these men are half as dangerous as you say, they're already near. Probably tracking you via your phone."

"Then maybe you should have tossed in onto a truck headed out of town instead of smashing it here like a caveman?"

Matt sighed. She was right. It'd been an impulsive move. He was trying to impress her with his strength but instead she now thought he was an untrustworthy meathead who didn't plan ahead. It was closer to the truth than he was comfortable with. The bear inside him wanted to claim her as his mate, it didn't understand why there was so much talking still happening when they both clearly lusted for each other. He should just sweep her off her feet, carry her back to his den, and spend the next fifty years mating and eating and mating until they were surrounded by so many cubs they couldn't even count them all.

"Is there anyone you can call?" Matt asked. But what he meant was, "do you have a boyfriend?"

"No," she shook her head, a darkness sliding into her eyes. "Not anymore."

"No one? Not parents or friends or siblings?"

"I don't want to drag them into this. The last person I told about all of this ended up dead at my feet. Do you think I want that for my sister?"

"Where does she live?"

"I can't tell you that."

Infuriating woman! How could he help her, how could he protect her, if she wouldn't tell him anything? He had to earn her trust, to show her that he wasn't some backwoods hick with sawdust between his ears.

"If I can get you out of here—get you to a safe place—will you tell me what's going on?"

The woman thought about it, chewing her plump lip in a way that made Matt's bear groan and roll over. He wanted to chew her lip. He wanted to tear her dress off to see what her nipples looked like. He wanted to hold her breasts in his hands and bury his face in their softness, licking and chewing her sensitive buds until she begged him to mate her.

"Okay," she said. "I don't know how else I'll get out of here alive. Take me someplace safe and I'll tell you everything."

"Fantastic," Matt said and grinned at her like she'd just agreed to go to prom with him.

"But first we need to find my car. I need to get something out of the glove box."

#

"Good thing for you my brother runs the only wrecker around. He towed your car to his shop. Just tell me what you need and he can bring it to us." The big man, Matt, said in a reassuring tone. He wasn't taking this seriously. Why did men never take Mina seriously? They saw her curves, her breasts, or maybe the color of her skin and assumed she was overreacting about everything. Mobsters killed her business partner while she watched. She was not overreacting.

"I can't do that." Mina placed her hands on the table and stood up, the effect would have been more intimidating if Matt wasn't the largest single person she'd ever seen. What would it feel like to have him wrapped around her? If you spooned with him, he'd be the whole silverware drawer. Mina never felt like a small woman—

genetics and a wicked sweet tooth had seen to that—but next to Matt she felt positively petite. Not for the first time since he'd walked in the door, she wondered how it would feel to be under him, to kick her heels to the sky for him.

The longer she was near him, the more intense the heat in her belly became. Just smelling him was making her ache with need. If she licked his skin, she might just melt. There was no time for thoughts like these. Keeping her phone had been a stupid mistake. She'd thought she needed it for maps and GPS to get to Oregon, but really it was probably a giant flashing dot telling Harker and his goons where she'd gone.

It was a miracle they weren't already there.

"Get me to my car. Take me someplace safe. And put some hot food in my belly, and I'll tell you everything."

Matt leaned back in the chair, lacing his fingers behind his head and showing off his massively muscled arms. Did he bench press trucks for fun? How did a county lawyer get built like that? "Hot food? Trying to sweeten the deal when I wasn't looking?" He smiled at her again, as if she was on a first date and not being hunted by killers. It was soothing and sexy and maddeningly inappropriate.

"A girl's got to eat," Mina shrugged.

"I should warn you, I'm a terrible cook. I can make three things."

"Microwave dinners, plain spaghetti, and toast?" Mina guessed.

When Matt laughed his whole body shook and his face filled with light. Mina really wanted to see that again. "You are not far off," he said. "I can make pancakes, omelettes, and a fantastic venison stew."

A Slice of Honeybear Pie

"What's your favorite food?" Mina asked. Looking at his body, she would have guessed he existed solely on egg whites and push-ups.

Matt's eyebrows shot up. "Oh man, now that is a difficult question. I like strawberries. And pancakes. A buttery grilled cheese with pickles is pretty nice. A big San Francisco burrito full of guacamole and sour cream and rice and cheese is always good. But I'd have to say that my all time favorite food of foods, would have to be pie."

"What kind of pie?" Mina sensed some leverage. The man had a taste for sweet things and if there was one thing she knew how to do better than anyone, it was make sweet things.

"Oh any kind of pie is great. Banana cream pie, strawberry pie, apple pie. Even a shepherd's pie is great, especially with buttery mashed potatoes on top."

"You ever tried honeybear pie?"

Matt's eyes sparkled with desire. He literally licked his lips and shook his head.

"You get me out of here and I will bake you the sweetest honeybear pie you've ever had."

Their eyes met and Mina could feel the electricity moving between them. She wanted him. Every atom of her body burned for him. It was bizarre. She'd never felt such overpowering attraction to anyone. She wanted him to rip her shirt off and lick honey off her breasts. She wanted him to bury his handsome mouth in her sex and devour her until her toes curled and she screamed to the heavens.

She needed to get the hell away from him.

"Give me two minutes," Matt said, then left the room.

Chapter 3
Bearly Keeping It Together

Heading to the car, Mina fought the urge to sprint off into the woods. Just being outside in the fresh air made her feel a thousand times better. She could run. She could always run. She might not get anywhere and the woods might be full of bears and rattlesnakes and Harker's men, but the illusion of freedom was a comfort.

She'd hoped that being out of the stuffy office-bedroom, being away from the amazing smell of Matt, would let her get her aching, yearning need for the man under control. Like maybe it was a chemical thing, and if she couldn't smell him she wouldn't feel the overpowering urge to drop her panties for him? But it was no use. He was in her. Well, not in her in her, but his scent was like a drug in her system and she wanted to rub her face all over his chest and smooth her fingers all over his hard muscles and open herself for him.

As the sun rose, Bearfield took Mina's breath away. The town was nestled in a crook near the top of a mountain, with the rolling valleys full of redwoods and sequoias stretching out in all directions. The sun broke over the distant mountains, casting russet shadows across the deep greens of the forest. Here and there below them, Mina could pick out rustic homes amongst the trees. Thin mountain roads wove their way across the face of the rock, almost invisible. This place held secrets.

Mina had always found the countryside alien. She'd grown up in Chicago, moved to San Francisco after college. She was a city girl in her bones. She'd seen the greatest cities of the world—New York, Tokyo, Barcelona, Paris. What could the countryside possible offer that was better?

A Slice of Honeybear Pie

She glanced over at Matt, standing by the police station door, soothing the old sheriff with his honeyed words and she had an idea of the sweet things the country hid. Maybe there were reasons to embrace other ways of life?

Matt smiled at the sheriff, clomped him on the back with one big hand and walked back over to where Mina stood next to the Jeep.

"He's not happy about this, but he's released you into my care. He'll hold off on filing charges or reports for twenty-four hours, but a wrecked car needs to be reported. The car has a vin number and anyone looking for you who has access to the system will know you were here." The man shrugged. "Just try not to commit any felonies for the next day or two, okay?"

"I can't make any promises." She meant it to come light and flirty, but there was a darkness in her tone she couldn't hide. If Harker's men came for her, she'd defend herself. She had no choice.

"Keep saying things like that," Matt said, "and I'll have to give you back to old Petey."

"Mina."

"Excuse me?"

"My name is Mina." She felt a heat rise in her cheeks as she said it.

"Mina," Matt said again, grinning at the name. "That's beautiful."

He opened the door for her like a gentleman, giving a slight nod to her as she clambered up into the seat. The car smelled like him in all the best possible ways. You can tell a lot about a person from the state of their car. Harker's car had been slick and shiny and silent, like a shark. He'd avoided any personal details inside so it always had that temporary feeling of a rental. Mina's car, if we're being honest, had always been a bit of a mess, with tissues and loose change and scribbled notes stuffed into the cupholders. Matt's Jeep was organized and clean, but still felt lived in. He had an old coffee mug on the floor emblazoned with the logo of someplace called the Bearfield Lodge. He had a stack of business cards with his name on them in a little plastic pocket affixed to the dash. The seat was cozy and the whole inside smelled like a pine forest and sex appeal, it made her dizzy every time she breathed in.

Matt swung into the Jeep in one practiced move. "My brother's salvage yard is just around the mountain from here," he said. "And it's near the grocery. Do you need anything special for this pie?"

Gangsters were after here, and this infuriating man was focused on the pie? "Do you have good apples?"

"Yep, from an orchard just down the river from here."

"Do you have flour and sugar and butter and salt?"

"Who doesn't?" he said. Harker doesn't, Mina knew. She should never have gotten into business with the man, let alone into his bed, after seeing his empty kitchen. He had salt and condiments and packaged ramen. The man was worth tens of millions, but he had no food in his house.

"The recipe gets its name from one of those little plastic bears full of honey. Do you have one of those?"

"No, but I have some pretty good honey." Matt grinned at her like he was telling a great joke. Then when she didn't laugh or smile back, he added, "I have a beehive out back of my property. Fresh honey, whenever you want it."

A Slice of Honeybear Pie

"That'll do," Mina said. She leaned her forehead against the cool glass of the window and watched Bearfield slowly reveal itself to her. "That'll do nicely."

# # #

They drove in silence for the first mile. Every time Matt opened his mouth to make small talk, Mina cut him off. "I'll tell you everything after we get the item from my car."

Her heart beat slower, her skin lost some of the tang of fear. She was calming down around him, but just a little.

"Okay, well then I'll talk. My brother's place, well, it's a bit shabby. Of the three of us he's the least interested in appearances. I swear, if we show up before noon and he's wearing clothes it'll be a miracle. We could always go get breakfast first and then come back once he's put himself together a bit?" His bear sat up and took notice at the mention of breakfast. They didn't always agree, his bear and him, but there were a few areas where they were in total harmony.

"Car first," Mina said, though the fire was out of her words. A wistfulness played in her eyes as she watched the trees and curves of the village fly past.

Matt fought to keep his eyes on the road. He wanted to watch her curves, to see the light that played in her eyes. He felt like he could spend a hundred years studying her face and never grow bored of it. What was this?

"When we show up and you see the full Michael Morrissey experience, don't say I didn't warn you."

Mina tore her gaze away from the hypnotic roll of the woods and fixed it on Matt. "Is he as big as you?"

"He's the runt of the family, but our brother Marcus is bigger than both of us."

"What's he do?"

"Construction, mostly. Living out here, the work isn't always steady, so a lot of guys have multiple gigs they work. Take Michael, for example. In any other town he'd just be a mechanic, but out here he's a mechanic and a wrecker driver and runs a salvage yard and refinishes furniture and sells gas on the side." Matt shrugged, "It's the country way."

"It's like running a restaurant," Mina offered. "You think at first you'll just be the chef, or maybe designing the menus, but then you find yourself hiring people and managing them. And you have to literally design your menus so that they can be printed out and actual people can read them. You have to source your ingredients and pay invoices and all of a sudden you realize it's been three weeks and you haven't cooked once."

"So that's what you do?" Matt asked, caution in his voice. "You run a restaurant."

"I used to. I was good at it, too. But then . . . " her voice trailed off. "I'll tell you more once we get the flash drive."

# # #

The sign above the salvage yard said, "Morrissey and Sons Salvage." The sign was a large plate of rusted metal with the words cut out of it in a slagged rough hand. Beyond the sign was a wooden shack that looked like it predated the gold rush with walls patched up with whatever was at hand at the time. Mina looked and saw a coffee can that had been pressed flat and affixed over a hole with glue and duct tape. The shack's exterior was rough and sloppy but the yard was neatly organized. She'd never seen a salvage operation before, but had imagined it like a towering junkyard full of cars and trash. The reality was more like a yard sale run by an obsessive.

Boxes and drawers and buckets stood in neat rows, each sporting a tidily hand-lettered sign explaining what was inside and listing a price. "Glass door knobs, $1." And, "Ancient Cell Phones, $2." And so on, forming hundreds of precise rows leading out from the shack like tiny soldiers on parade. Not a single screw was out of place and not a single speck of trash marred the grassy lawn.

The door to the shack flew open and out strode the second largest man Mina had ever seen. He was naked but for a pair of work boots and aviator sunglasses perched on his handsome, aquiline nose. The man's body was impossible to take in all at once, and not just because he was so big. Michael Morrissey was shorter than his brother, Matthew, but also not nearly as wide. The man had a more compact build and sandy blonde hair. Streaks of grease and dirt marked his well-muscled delicious body almost like tiger stripes. Mina tried hard not to stare at his cock, but it was impossible not to. The man was HUNG, there was no better way to say it. No wonder he walked around naked all the time.

"Matt," the naked man nodded, sipping coffee out of a *world's sexiest grandma* mug loudly. "The car's out back. Help yourself to it but let me know if it's a junker. She's got some good bones under all that flash. I could really have some fun with it." Michael's eyes sparkled darkly as he spoke, fixed on Mina's. She knew he wasn't talking about the car and felt a mixture of heat at being so openly admired and anger at being treated like something the guy could call dibs on.

"Mikey, put some damn clothes on. There's a lady present."

"I know," the younger brother smirked, "that's why I'm naked." He sipped his coffee again then turned and went back into his junkyard shack, giving Mina a very full view of his taut, perfectly sculpted rear end. Only when the door closed did Mina finally exhale. She hadn't even realized she'd been holding her breath.

Matt sighed loudly, in that way every older brother did when confronted with the shenanigans of his younger, cooler brother. "Let's go around back. That's where he keeps the cars."

Mina followed Matt's lead, picking her way between the neatly spaced buckets of staplers and picture frames and drawer pulls. She couldn't help herself from watching her attorney's ass as he walked. Would he look as good naked? Could that even be possible? Michael was possibly the hottest man she'd ever laid eyes on in person. She had no doubt from the glint in his eyes that if she turned up on his doorstep he would take her in and rock her world until the sun came up. First Harker, then Matt and now his brother.

Why was her life all of a sudden full of beautiful, crazy men?

"You say your other brother is even bigger than you two?"

A prickliness radiated from Matt. "Yeah, the guy is like twice my size. He can't even fit in a normal car. He has all his shoes special made by a blacksmith. He doesn't even wear normal clothes, just a tent with a belt around it." He turned back and smiled at her.

"Oh ha ha," she said, sticking her tongue out at him and then laughing.

"My god you have a sexy laugh," Matt said.

Mina felt the heat rush back into her. Being around this man was dangerous. If she got through the day with her panties intact it would be a miracle. What was going on with her? It was like there was a connection between them, deep in her bones, boiling in her blood.

She was saved from tearing her clothes off and begging him to have his way with her by the sight of her poor battered and squashed car. "Oh no, the poor thing. What have I done to you?" She ran to her car and ran her hand along the dented top.

"You're lucky to have survived this," Matt said. He walked around the car and inspected it for danger. "The corner where you lost control, we've been trying to get a sign up there for years. You're not the first tourist to go over the edge. Not even the second this year alone."

The doors were horribly bent and completely impossible to open. The windshield was shattered but in place. The whole car looked like it'd been stepped on by a giant and then kicked down a hill and then rubbed all over with scouring pads.

"This was my first car." Mina patted the hood affectionately, like she was saying good bye to a favorite dog. "I bought it when I made head pastry chef at *Sweet Surrender.*" She bent over and kissed the hood. It was like a friend was dead because of her negligence. The tears she'd been holding back for days finally erupted, spilling down her cheeks in a scalding rain.

"I was so stupid," she began.

A Slice of Honeybear Pie

Matt stepped forward, concern furrowing his big handsome brow. He gathered her up in his strong arms and let her talk while holding her close.

Mina eased herself into the incredible warmth of the man, feeling his strength wrapped around her she felt free to speak for the first time since it'd happened.

"His name was Harker. He seduced me. He said he loved me, that he needed me, that we were destined to be together. I should have run back then, but I was stupid. I was so amazed that anyone as handsome and successful as him could love a fat girl like me that I gave in."

"Why would you think you were fat?" Matt murmured into the top of her head. "You're absolutely gorgeous."

The heat flared again inside Mina, turning liquid and dripping through her.

"I worked my way up the chef ladder for years, paying my dues, putting in the stupid hours you need to as a pastry chef just starting out and then the even worse hours as head pastry chef at one of the fanciest brunch places in the city."

Whenever she said *brunch* Matt's belly rumbled. It was adorable, like there was a wild animal inside him grumbling for treats.

"And then I did what every chef does when they reach the top and get sick of the hours and the pay. I started my own business. A cute little patisserie and brunch place." Another growl against Mina's cheek made her smile, the tears were gone now. "And it failed. Spectacularly. I made so many rookie mistakes. The menu was too big, the staff were—never mind, it's not important. But I lost everything when it folded, my entire savings, and I had to go crawling back to *Sweet*

Surrender to get my job back. It would have taken me
years to get the funding together to try again, if the bank
would even gamble on me again. I was desperate." Mina
sank deeper into Matt's embrace.

"And that's when he showed up?" Matt rumbled.

"That's when he showed up. Harker. Like the devil
himself he arrived, whisking me off my feet. He'd been
upset that my restaurant had closed and wanted to make
another go of it. His office was just across the street, you
see, and the idea of a wonderful little breakfast place
where he could get amazing pastries and fresh coffee and
take clients was extremely appealing to him."

"What's this Harker guy do?"

"He told me he was a business man. A venture
capitalist. He sought out struggling businesses and
invested in them to bring them to their full potential and

got paid handsomely for it. He was aiming at making

billionaire before he turned forty, he said."

"I know you can't see my face right now, Mina, but

let me assure you I am rolling my eyes so damn hard

right now."

"None of it was true. Well, he did seek out struggling

businesses, that's true. And he was trying to make

billionaire, sure. But the part about helping? He and his

goons don't care about helping. It's all a scam. They

have a thousand different schemes running at once, like

some Silicon Valley version of the mafia. Money

laundering and fake names on the time sheets and

falsifying receipt of goods. I didn't understand half of

what they were doing."

"So you took him up on it?"

"A handsome man told me he loved me, that I could

be beautiful if I just lost some weight, that I could be

successful if I just did everything he asked. He built me up with one breath and tore me down with the next. I was powerless."

A low growl rumbled in the big man's throat. "I don't like men who prey on women."

"We opened a new establishment. And though we started with my vision for it, piece by piece everything I loved was replaced by Harker's ideas until my charming French-inspired pastry-focused brunch place that was affordable and paid workers well and wanted to source every ingredient I possibly could locally became something else. Harker's vision was cold. He treated people like a game, always looking for some weakness to exploit, preying on their fears. He bullied the staff and stole from them, changing their timecards on a whim and fining them for every imagined slight. Wearing the wrong kind of shoes was a ten dollar fine. If a waitress didn't show enough skin, she was fined twenty dollars. If a table sat unbussed for more than three minutes, the busboy was fired. And so on."

"He sounds like a real asshole."

"Which is all I thought he was, at first. But then one night I was working late and my right-hand man, Francis, came to me." Mina's throat closed as she said his name, her words escaping in a whisper. She wanted to tell Matt everything but she didn't know if she physically could. "Francis helped with everything. He was darling with the staff and gracious with the customers and a catty little bitch once the closed sign went up and the wine came out. If he'd been straight I would have married him years ago. But alas." Tears burned again in her eyes.

Matt made soothing sounds. Distantly she was aware that they still were in a junkyard on top a mountain, and that Harker's goons were still after her. But with Matt protecting her she didn't care.

"One night, one of Harker's minions had left a laptop behind. We'd had a surprise health inspection and Harker's men had to clear out the back before they were discovered. It was all pretty routine. But they'd left behind a computer, which was so unlike them. His guys were careful to the point of paranoia. And Francis knew something was wrong. He'd worked in dirty kitchens before and knew when the books were being cooked. So he took the computer home. He saw only a fraction of their plans, but it was horrible. Harker was into so much more than we knew. He bought apartment buildings in the Mission and then hired men to burn them down so he could evict the residents. He bought city supervisors. He was into every illegal activity you could imagine.

Francis put everything damning on a thumb drive and brought it to me. He wanted me to take it to the police."

"Why wouldn't he do it himself?"

"He had priors from a long time ago, plus being gay and Filipino made him used to being ignored by the cops. He brought me the drive, told me what was on it and then, the next time I saw him, he was dead."

"I'm so sorry," Matt said, his arms holding her tighter.

"We met at the restaurant to discuss what we were going to do. I was totally in denial. Harker had my head spinning, always praising my work then attacking me for not losing weight fast enough. He told me he wanted to marry me." Matt's arms flexed around Mina in irritation, surprising her with the protectiveness she sensed in the man. "But that he couldn't until he knew I'd look great in a wedding dress."

A Slice of Honeybear Pie

"You would look amazing in a wedding dress right now," Matt murmured.

"So when Francis came to me, I thought there must be a mistake. I told him we should take the data to Harker and demand an explanation, but we didn't even get to have that conversation. Harker was waiting for us. I don't know if he had me followed or if he had my phone tapped or what, but he knew. He and his goons stormed in while we were talking. The man was unrecognizable with fury, ranting and smashing things with his bare hands, screaming about how we jeopardized everything. It was insane. He was barely human."

Matt stiffened as if he knew something, but didn't speak, so Mina continued.

"And Francis, may he rest in peace, never had any patience for bullies. So when Harker starts flipping out and screaming and smashing tables, Francis just starts in berating the man for being a criminal and a low-life and scum. And that's when Harker pulled out his gun and shot Francis." The tears came for real now, a flood that felt like it was never going to stop. She had more to say, more to tell Matt. But the words were choked off by the raging river inside her. She wanted to tell him that being next to him was the first time she'd felt safe in years. She wanted to say that they'd only just met, but she felt a primal connection between them. But she sensed that he knew already.

Matt let her cry, to his credit. He didn't shush her or tell her it wasn't worth crying about. He held her tight and let her grief crash against him, taking all she could throw. And when she was done all he said was, "Where's this flash drive?" as he handed her his clean white handkerchief.

A Slice of Honeybear Pie

Mina dried her eyes and wiped her nose and wished he wasn't seeing her this way, not that Matt seemed to care. "In the glove compartment, under some papers."

Matt squeezed his head and an arm into the car through the passenger-side window. She heard metal screaming as it bent and plastic crunching. The big man emerged with the drive held between two fingers like he'd just performed a magic trick.

"That's it!" Mina said.

"I'll take that, if you don't mind," came a growling voice from the shadows of Michael's shack. A man stepped forward, one of Harker's goons. Carlisle, she thought his name was. Or maybe Quint? All of Harker's men had a look about them, with shaved heads and dull eyes and a smell of the sea that clung to them at all times.

"I don't think you will," Matt replied, shoving the flash drive into Mina's hands.

"Matt, just give it to him. He's got a gun."

"Indeed I do," the thug smiled, showing off a wide mouth full of very white teeth and a silver handgun with a long silencer on the end. "And here's how it works." The thug aimed at Matt and fired before Mina could even scream. He fired nine times, each like a bass drum thumping.

"He's got a gun," Matt rumbled. "But I have a *bear.*" The thug looked surprised as the man charged him, glancing down at his gun like he expected it to say "Toy Gun, Not Real" on the side. Matt took the distance between them in five loping steps then jumped in the air . . .

And came down on top of the man as a giant golden bear with the tattered rags of Matt's second best suit clinging to its paws and neck. The bear that was Matt roared with a force that shook Mina's teeth and set off a car alarm somewhere else in the junkyard.

Michael came running out of the shack, now dressed in jeans and a hooded sweatshirt.

"Jesus, Matt!" Michael yelled. "Don't kill the guy. It's not worth it. Don't do this."

The thug was unconscious, trapped under the several tons of bear that had landed on him. But he wasn't dead. At least not yet.

"Go inside before someone sees you," Michael's eyes were wide with panic. "What the hell were you thinking, transforming in front of her?"

The bear that was also Matt looked back at Mina, like he'd forgotten she was there. He had the same eyes, Matt's eyes. They looked forlornly at Mina and she felt a great wave of sympathy well up inside her matched only by the wonderment at exactly what the hell was going on.

Matt-the-bear huffed and grumbled, he was easily larger than her car and when he moved his flesh shook as the massive slabs of muscle shifted under his fur. The morning sun caught his golden coat just right and for a moment he was surrounded by a honeyed light that took Mina's breath away. She thought she had secrets, that she had something to hide. Her problems felt small next to the giant werebear.

"Go, go inside. Get some clothes for yourself." Michael slapped the bear on the haunches and the big animal rambled inside. The handsome man turned to Mina, "You probably have some questions."

"Matt turned into a bear." Her voice came slow, like the words didn't make sense in the order she was putting them in.

"That's not a question."

"Matt turned into a bear?" she said, her voice lilting upwards at the end.

"Yes."

"Are you a bear, too?"

Michael nodded. "Oh yes."

"Is everyone in this town secretly a bear?"

"I can't answer that. I can only speak for Matt and myself."

Mina blinked in the sunlight. She had so many questions, but couldn't grasp any of them long enough to ask them. "Is he dangerous?"

"Not to you."

"Why not to me?"

Michael smiled at her, every trace of his smirk gone in an instant. "Can't you feel it? You're his mate."

Matt emerged from the tumble-down shack. He was wearing Michael's clothes and they fit him snugly, the sweatpants and Winnie-the-Pooh t-shirt outlining every muscle in the man's body.

"Dang, bro, that's my favorite shirt and you're going to stretch the hell out of it."

"I'll get you another one," Matt warned.

"They don't make them anymore. Limited edition, homes."

"Then I'll get one off eBay. We have more important things to worry about than your ironic bear shirts." He turned to Mina. "We need to get you some place safe. There will be more of them. Much more."

"What do I do with this guy?" Michael asked, poking the unconscious goon with a toe.

"Hold him some place safe. We can turn him over to the authorities once we deal with his boss."

Michael nodded, then picked up the thug with one hand, slinging him over his shoulder like a bag of laundry before walking down through his junkyard, through the fence, and down a hidden path into the bones of the mountain.

"Do you trust me?" Matt turned to Mina. "I need to know."

"He shot you."

"Yes."

"Did he miss?"

"No."

"Does it hurt?"

"Not even a little."

"Are you going to hurt me?"

"Never. I swear by the sleeping fathers of the rock, I will never hurt you, Mina."

"Then let's go."

Jacqueline Sweet

Chapter 4
Bearly Made It

"How does this work? You just like flex and change?"

Mina was trying to understand, but her mind didn't want to. It was like grasping at smoke. The idea of a man who was also a bear, it was preposterous and yet she'd seen it with her own eyes. Or had she? After the junkyard attack they'd driven straight to Matt's house, the big man taking the curves of the mountain at breakneck speed. He could do that. He grew up there. Mina wanted to know more, to discuss what had just happened, but Matt made it clear he couldn't talk when he was being very careful about not driving off the edge of the world.

Instead she thought about Harker's man. If one of them was here, they all were. He had dozens of goons. Bearfield wasn't that big. They'd find her. But running wasn't an option either. There was one road into town and one road out. They'd surely be watching both.

Her thoughts jumped from bears to Harker to bears and back again to Harker, neither topic comfortable enough to ponder overlong. So for the rest of the ride she planned out the pie she'd bake Matt as thanks for all his help. "In fairy tales," her mother used to say, "no one ever says I love you. They give food and they kiss. That's what love is made of."

Matt's house was nestled deep in the woods, down a long winding dirt driveway that dropped away on either side precipitously into the thick forest. Built of redwood timber, the home nearly glowed with warmth. Mina caught her breath when she saw it. It was a modern take on a log cabin, with giant windows overlooking the surrounding wilderness. It stood three stories tall, at least, with the lower level partially hidden beneath the underbrush. She'd been worried. It could have looked like Michael's shack—indefensible and tacky and lazy. But it was as far from the tumbledown shack as could be.

A small part of her whispered, *wouldn't it be nice to live here? To make a life here?* But she pushed that hopeful thought away. She just met Matt Morrissey. It was too soon to be thinking about a life with him. The last time she'd jumped when a man called had been Harker and that was still unraveling all around her.

"What do you think?" Matt asked, trying to hide the concern in his eyes. What was he worried about? He was a giant bulletproof bear. He'd be fine. Mina, on the other hand . . .

"It's gorgeous. It looks very cozy."

Relief washed across Matt's face. "It's certainly that. I'm a bear, and bears love comfort."

"Michael's place didn't look very cozy."

"That's not his real home. My little brother spends more time as a bear than as a man. He has a den out back of his junkyard that's his real home."

"That's why he's always naked," Mina realized.

"That is exactly why he's always naked," Matt agreed. "Let me show you around."

The tour didn't have the air of let's-find-a-defensible-corner that Mina had been expecting. In fact, Matt hardly seemed worried at all. Instead it felt like he was pitching her on the house, proposing *something*. As he showed off the bathrooms with antique Victorian fixtures supplied by his younger brother and the energy saving modifications built by his older brother, he was more like realtor than a protector. Or like a suitor. Michael had said she was his mate. He was showing off his den to his potential mate. Mina grew dizzy at the thought. She was a fat girl from the wrong side of Chicago. Girls like her didn't get things like this. It wasn't on the menu.

"Tell me something," Mina said, interrupting Matt's honestly-not-that-interesting discussion of how he built the guest bedroom floors by hand. "You live alone."

"Yes?"

"No secret wives or girlfriends or doddering old mothers around?"

"Just me." Matt cocked his head. "Where are you going with this line of questioning, councillor?"

"You built a five-bedroom, six bath home by yourself in the middle of the woods."

He nodded. "And you want to know why a guy who lives alone builds a house this size?"

"I do. I really do. Do you plan to sell it? Are you going to turn it into a B&B? I'm sure you could make a killing at it, though you'd need to improve that driveway. You wouldn't want any sleep-deprived tourists rolling their cars off the edge."

"Could mean more business for Michael. He always needs the money."

"How can you afford this? It's too big. It's too much." What was she doing? He was protecting her, keeping her safe at his home, but she knew he wasn't saying everything. What if he was another Harker with devious plans? What if he wanted to make her fall in love with him just to rip the rug out from under her when he got bored with the novelty of dating a curvy girl like her?

A Slice of Honeybear Pie

"My family has owned this corner of the mountain since forever," he shrugged. "I felled my own wood with my own two hands. I worked with my brothers to plain the wood and treat it. It took a long time." Matt leaned against the frame of the guest bedroom. The doors were all bigger than usual, built for a man of his size. They made Mina feel small in a way she found appealing. "I don't like lying, Mina. I don't like dancing around the truth."

"But you're an attorney."

"I'm not a trial lawyer. I help people with their wills and deeds and that sort of thing. But look, here's what I'm trying to say and I apologize if it freaks you out."

"It's freaking me out," Mina backed away across the bedroom. She realized there were no other exits, except the bathroom and a window with a twenty foot drop. Matt blocked her only way out of the room. He had the keys. He had her isolated in the woods, miles from anyone else.

Matt sniffed the air and a wounded expression creased his big handsome face. It hurt Mina's heart to see the pain so plain.

"Let's go down to the kitchen," Matt said. "I can say my piece after we've eaten." His belly rumbled in agreement and Mina wondered for the first time if it was his stuck or the bear inside him making the noise.

# # #

For a guy who didn't know how to cook more than three things, Matt kept a well-stocked kitchen.

"Tell me how it works," Mina said, a giant Matt-sized sandwich clutched in her fingers. Seeing her in his home—in the home he built for her—brought an electricity to Matt's blood. He wanted to impress her. He wanted to charm her. But every time he started to open up, he smelled the fear explode from Mina's skin. She was terrified, of this Harker guy, sure, but also of Matt. He needed to fix that.

"It's like the bear always wants to come out and I just have to let it." He shrugged, making himself two giant sandwiches with spicy mustard and swiss cheese and lettuce and cranberry sauce. "But also if I get really angry, it comes out. Its important for us bear shifters to stay calm and happy as much as possible. It's one of the reasons we all live in the country, away from crowds of people. Isolation helps. Quiet helps. Being free of the city stresses helps. But sometimes you just need to bear out and see the world through bear eyes."

Mina shook her head. "I still don't understand how you can protect me. These guys have guns. Guys with guns kill bears everyday. And I'd hate for anything to happen to you, I really would." Her eyes sparkled as she said it. When she ate, the woman glowed. Her guarded expression melted away to reveal the even more stunning Mina beneath the shield. "This is really good," she said, nodding at the sandwich. A dab of cranberry sauce clung to her lower lip and just as Matt reached out to wipe it away, she licked the sauce and grazed his thumb with her hot little tongue. Matt felt like he'd been struck by lightning, like a circuit connecting his thumb to his now half-hard cock had been completed.

He couldn't wait to claim her, to mate her. Why did these gangster pricks have to get in the way?

"I can protect you. I really can. Let me prove it to you, yeah?" The urge to show off, to perform for his mate was overwhelming. The man and the bear both craved her approval on a visceral level. Wolves might steal a mate and force themselves onto her, but a bear never would. Matt searched around his airy, expansive kitchen until he found his knife block. He selected one of the biggest sharpest knives. "Here's a chef's knife."

"It's actually a santoku. The chef's knife is one more slot up."

Matt laughed. He wasn't used to being corrected, but he liked it. He wanted a mate who was sharp, who was intelligent, who would make him a better man, who would challenge him. He'd seen men settle for the first woman who could put up with them, the first woman who was comfortable to be around, and it never ended well. Marcus had done that, and look at how miserable he was. A man needed a partner in life, someone to force him to grow and strive and be better.

"Just take the knife please." Matt handed it to her like a knight presenting his sword to his king.

"I don't think I like where this is going."

"Just trust me," Matt flashed his best smile, the one that caught everyone off guard with its warmth.

Mina narrowed her eyes at him. "Okay, fine. What do I do?"

Matt backed up across the room ten feet and spread his arms wide. "Throw the knife at me."

"What? No. No! Are you crazy?" And then Mina's face darkened as she entertained the possibility that he might be crazy. She'd seen him bear out, but that wasn't enough. The magic that let him change had a defense mechanism. A sort of disbelief that came when anyone saw the shift. Most people ran screaming when they saw it, but even afterwards they wouldn't recall that Matt had changed in front of them. Their memories would be hazy, clouded by terror and magic. Mates were different though. As were any blood kin. Certain other people had a natural immunity to the terror for some reason Matt had never figured out. But even with mates, it took a gradual process of easing them into the knowledge or they'd just forget. If Matt didn't show Mina his hidden self often enough, it'd fade away from Mina's memory like a dream.

"No weapon forged by man can pierce my skin or rob me of my breath," Matt intoned with a voice like a cartoon wizard. "At least that's what they say."

"I'll aim for an arm," Mina said. "That way if you're crazy I at least don't kill you."

"If you kill me, the house is yours though."

"Maybe I should aim for your head then."

"Please do, it won't matter."

"I'm really not comfortable with this, Matt." Hearing her say his name put a fizz in his bones. He could listen to his name on her lips for the rest of his life, especially if they were parted and slick and moaning it over and over again.

Matt shook his head. The mating impulse was overpowering. "Wait, before you throw it let me change out of these clothes. Michael would be pissed if I got a knife wound in his Pooh Bear shirt." He peeled off the shirt and stood half naked and exposed in front of her. Mina stared at him like he was an oncoming train.

"Okay, throw the knife."

Mina stared, eyes wide. The knife dangled absently from her fingers.

"I'm ready. Throw it!" Matt jumped up and down, excited to show off his trick. But Mina was frozen. He sniffed the air, and caught her scent. Lust, overpowering, knee-shaking lust. Her heart raced in her chest. Her breath came quick and shallow. Her pupils were dilated so that her warm brown eyes were almost entirely black.

Every one of his heightened animal senses told him that she was ready to mate, that her body was making itself ready for him, that she craved everything he had to offer.

He could take her. Right then, on the polished wood of the kitchen island, he could sweep the food to the floor and spread her open on the table. He could lick the honey from between her legs with long slow deliberate licks until her toes curled and she cried out his name. How would she sound when her pleasure took her? Would she scream or whimper? Would she moan low and deep? Would she be one of those quiet girls who came in a chirping squeak? He needed to know.

And then Matt's phone buzzed, breaking the spell. Goddamn technology.

Mina looked down at the counter. "It's Michael. He says twenty dudes came by the junkyard looking for me."

There was no time for mating.

"We should run," Mina said. "We could make our way through the woods."

"How long could we run for? If we stand and fight them, this ends now. If you run, it only ends when you make a mistake."

"I don't want you to get hurt."

"No weapon forged can hurt me, remember?"

Mine chewed her lip and studied the knife. "No weapon forged? So what about like a tree branch? Or a meteor? Or a really big fall?"

Matt laughed. She was so quick, so fast on her feet. "It takes most bears weeks—if not years—to see the loophole. But yeah, I'm not invulnerable. When the ancient men who would become my ancestors made their pact with the great bear spirit, the bear promised them protection from all weapons and the man promised the bear their knowledge and cunning." He shrugged.

"Let me get this straight, you're saying *the entire natural world is your kryptonite?*"

"Well when you put it like that it doesn't sound so impressive."

"It's still impressive, kind of." Mina narrowed her eyes as she thought, she rested one hand on her hip and Matt's temperature crept up as his eyes took in her fullness again. What would it feel like to bury himself in all of that softness? To roll around and kiss and nuzzle and thrust into it? "How does the magic know? How can it know whether a tree branch was naturally sharp or sharpened to be a spear by a man?"

"Spirits?" Matt offered with a grin and shrug. "Honestly, I don't have the answers beyond the stories my pop-pop told me."

"What if you choked on like a plastic toy? I mean, it's forged by man but not a weapon. Would it kill you or just turn to ash or what?"

"Just throw the knife, Mina."

"I don't think I want to. What if you're crazy?"

He fixed her with his best bear stare and let the beast into his eyes for a moment. "Throw the knife," he growled, his voice shaking the glasses in his cabinets as if ten trucks were driving by.

In one sharp motion, Mina hurled the knife forward. *She's a chef,* Matt remembered, *of course she can throw a knife.* It flew straight and true at his chest at whip-crack speed. If he'd been a mortal man, he would've been dead. On some level, she must have believed him or she would have thrown wide. When the point of the knife harmlessly bounced off his naked chest with a whisper, whizzing off to clang against a chair, an end table, and finally the floor, Mina raced to look at him. She peered at his skin, running her fingers over his chest.

"There's not even a scratch."

"And there never will be."

At her touch, electricity spread across his skin.

"Wow," Mina said, looking up at him with her huge brown eyes. "Do you feel this, too?"

"Yes," Matt whispered, cupping her chin in his hand.

"What's going on?" she asked, lips parted, eyes closed, stretching on her tiptoes up to reach his lips.

"You're my mate, Mina. We're destined for each other."

"That's what Harker told me. Said we were fated to be together forever."

Matt smelled the men before he heard them. Gun oil. Saltwater. Fresh blood. He barely had time to curl himself around Mina before the front door burst in and the sound of gunfire roared in his ears. He felt the thumping of bullets against his flesh, like being struck with a hammer. He'd overstated his invulnerableness to Mina somewhat. Sure, bullets couldn't kill him, but they still hurt like the devil.

Chapter 5

Bearly Survived

In one moment, Mina went from admiring the carved muscular chest of the man protecting her, fingers tracing the stark ridges where his muscles curved and dipped, to cowering in fear under him as the world exploded around her. Splinters of wood exploded all around her. The far window shattered into a thousand points of light. All of Matt's beautiful, probably-hand-made furniture was destroyed in an instant. Mina should have been terrified, but instead she was furious.

How dare Harker come at her like this? She'd done everything he asked, had dieted for him, had changed her business into something cold and soulless for him, and it still wasn't enough. The man had to find more beautiful things in the world to ruin, because he had under it all a very ugly soul.

The gunfire stopped. The air hung thick with smoke and sawdust. The smell of the guns was improbably foul, a chokingly putrid smell that Mina hoped wouldn't linger long. Crouched under Matt, she couldn't see the men but she could hear footsteps. The slow *clunk clunk clunk* of Harker as he approached. He'd always loved these ridiculous boots with silver heels, like a cowboy who'd struck it rich and just had to show off.

"Miss Brooks, are you hiding under all that hillbilly?" Harker said with a sneer so severe you could hear it in his voice.

"Just let me go, Harker. I don't want to make trouble for you. Just take your men and get out." Mina peeked around Matt, saw Harker and at least a dozen of his bald, smelly goons.

A Slice of Honeybear Pie

The man's face twisted with anger. He was handsome—devastatingly so—when he tried, but when the real Harker surfaced his inner ugliness showed like a knife in a nursery. "You don't tell *me* what to do!" he roared. "You're nothing! Nothing at all! You don't get to jeopardize the plan. Not you."

"I'll even give you the flash drive. You can take it, Harker. Just get out of here and leave us be. You'll never see or hear from me again."

"It's a good deal, man. You should take it," Matt rumbled, his voice shaking her bones.

"I'm not afraid of you, little bear." Harker laughed. "You think you're the first shifter I've met? The first I've killed? She's my mate, not yours. We're fated. I can feel it."

"What kind of shifter are you?" Matt asked. He didn't move, just kept himself as a shield between Mina and the men who would harm her. "I can smell you're not human, but I don't recognize it."

Mina watched, peering around Matt, as Harker loosened his tie and shook himself free of his suit jacket and shirt. She remembered how she'd been amazed at his body, the sleek lines of his muscles, the smooth hardness of his flesh. But he'd always been cold against her. A man should be warm. A man should be caring. A man should be like Matt.

Harker's face twisted, his nose elongating and then his face stretching forward to meet his nose giving him a bullet-headed appearance. His teeth multiplied and blurred as rows of razored fangs dropped into place. And then Harker's eyes rolled over white as his skin took on a grubby gray color.

"Mina, do you remember what I said happened to my last girlfriend?"

"Of course, she died just before we met. A shark attack while snorkeling in Hawaii. You were really broken up about it."

"The part I kinda sorta forgot to mention was that *I was the shark*." Harker's body shifted and swelled, his legs remained man-sized and out of place with his bulging shark-shifter torso. He was part man and part shark and still a total jerk.

"Mina, get behind the counter," Matt whispered to her. "When I move, get there. It's a solid chunk of redwood. It'll stop any stray bullets and flying bodies."

"Flying bodies?" Mina asked, but then Matt was moving and she leapt for the safety of the standing counter, the kind of table her mother always called a "cooking island." Her knees slid across the wooden floor slick with sawdust and splintered wood. Across the room, Matt blurred and leapt and a great golden bear came down heavy of three of Harker's men. The entire house shook with the impact, dishes rattling off shelves, picture frames leaping off walls. Matt had spent so many years building the house, but she knew that he'd destroy it in an instant if it meant saving her.

The redwood counter shook and a body went flying over the top, spinning through the air. One of the goons. What could make you think it was a good idea to get into a fist fight with a magic bear? Did Harker pay them that much, or was the alternative a mysterious shark attack on dry land?

Matt roared at Harker and the shark shifter barked back with a choked, sputtering sound. Mina grabbed a shiny pan off the ground and held it so she could watch the fight in the reflection. The goons were all down or fled, now it was just the bear and the shark, facing off. Matt swiped at the gangster with his giant clawed paws and Harker snapped at the man's limb, nearly catching it in his teeth. *No weapon forged*, but a shark's teeth definitely weren't forged. Could Harker hurt matt? Could Harker *kill* Matt? It was unthinkable, but here she was thinking it.

The two of them seemed evenly matched. Harker snapped his jaws forward, nearly missing Matt. Matt cuffed him across the head, but Harker didn't even notice. It was up to Mina. She had to help. Matt couldn't do it alone. What did he know about fighting? He was a backwoods attorney with an amazing body, a sweet tooth, and a stunning house that was half splinters. Harker was a killer. Harker was experienced. It was only a matter of time before Harker won.

Unless Mina helped.

She should have been terrified, shaking in her dress, whimpering and sobbing, but she was just mad. She'd done so much for Harker, and now he was going to do something for her. He was going to lose.

What did she know about sharks? She knew the obvious things—fish, flippers, total a-holes, not as cool as dolphins, the movie *Jaws*—but none of it seemed useful. She couldn't exactly find a Sheriff Brody in the kitchen to help her out. She couldn't stuff an air tank or whatever down Harker's throat and then blow it up. She didn't know if that'd work, anyway. Harker's eyes rolled over white as he launched himself at Matt, knocking the big man across the room, landing on top of the bear and snapping at his face.

Smell. Sharks used smell to hunt. They couldn't use their eyes, cause they did the creepy doll eyes flip-over-white thing. So they used scent to hunt. Mina dashed around the redwood counter, and rifled through Matt's cupboards. As a chef, when she was in a kitchen she always paid attention to where things were. It was second nature, she didn't even realize she was doing it. First she grabbed a large empty jar. Then she went to the spices, fishing out the cayenne and chili powder and especially the mace. She dumped all of it into the jar held her hand over the top, and then raced across the room to where Harker had Matt trapped in a corner. Matt was on his feet again, but had nowhere to move. He couldn't even get a proper swipe in he was so boxed in by the room's corner. Harker gnashed his teeth and chomped forward blindingly fast, again and again, getting nothing more than a mouthful of fur.

Matt couldn't hold out much longer.

Mina ran up to Harker.

Matt saw her and shifted back to human form in the blink of an eye. "Mina, no!" Matt yelled, his eyes wide with panic.

Harker turned to face her, his massive shark head darting forward reflexively to take a bite out of her.

Time slowed down. Matt jumped at Harker to tackle the shifter. Harker slid through the air, eyes white, his jaws full of hundreds of triangular teeth stretching wide enough to swallow Mina whole. And Mina took her hand off the jar and tossed the spicy contents straight into the shark's wide nostrils.

The effect was instantaneous. One moment there was a shark man about to devour Mina and the next Harker was rolling around on the ground, in human form, clawing at his face and screeching like a demon. Every cook at some point gets a little cayenne in her eyes, a little chili power in her nose. At the culinary academy, it was a standard prank to have the new students sniff unlabeled spices to identify them and you never forgot what it was like to get a nose full of fresh powdered mace.

Matt shifted again, the bear taking the place of the man one more. He swiped with one giant paw and Harker stopped screeching and kicking. The shark's body was still.

It was over.

Mina threw herself on the big fuzzy bear and sobbed with relief. It was over. It was finally over. No more running. No more living in fear of Harker. No more bending herself to his will and dieting and playing along out of the misguided notion that he was the best she could hope for.

The fur under her cheek shifted and suddenly she found herself cradled in the airs of a very sweaty, very hot, very naked Matt. He kissed the top of her head and held onto her for as long as he could.

Chapter 6
Bearly Begun

While Matt swept up broken glass and bullets and shattered furniture from around the house, Mina busied herself in the kitchen. She'd promised the man a pie and Mina took her promises very seriously, especially when it came to baking.

The big insanely handsome man had calls to make before they cold relax and it was either bake, get in the way, or hide in a corner or fret. So of course it was honeybear pie time. Mina made the crust first. It wasn't her best effort, but she also didn't want to spend all day on it. She made the easiest crust she knew and placed the ball of dough, wrapped in plastic wrap, in Matt's freezer to chill. She balanced it on top of a stack of frozen pizzas and microwave burritos. When she moved in, all of this would be gone. No more frozen junk food, just honest cooking.

Were they mates? Were they fated? Or was this just an intense attraction that would fade in six months? She didn't know. Maybe it didn't matter? It felt amazing and Harker was gone, why not try something new? Her old patterns hadn't done her any good, had they?

On the phone, Matt argued with his brother Marcus about getting the windows replaced. Then made another call, to someone else, about dealing with the bodies.

Mina found the apples and sliced a disc out of one to taste it. Matt was right. They were perfect. Some artisanal blend. The hills of Northern California were lousy with them. Varietals you've never heard of, planted by people who didn't know they were supposed to graft apples, nit plant them, and ended up lucky anyway. She sliced ten apples into paper-thin discs, then tossed them in a large wooden bowl with flour and cinnamon and cloves and a hint of nutmeg. Then she found his honey in a high cupboard over the sink. It was in a giant earthenware jug that would have made Pooh Bear whine with jealousy. It must have weighed fifty pounds. There was no way she could move the jar. Heck, she could hardly reach it. The kitchen had been designed for a giant like Matt, not a woman like her. She'd need a step stool or a carpenter to make the kitchen usable. Thankfully the honey jar had a spigot, recessed but functional in the bottom edge of the jar. She held up a tablespoon and filled it with the glowing amber goodness.

Honey was tricky to cook with. You needed to be very careful when you sourced it. Under the sweetness, a refined palate could taste the notes of whatever the bees got into. Too often honey carried notes of heavy metals, of pesticides, of the weirdly beefy taste of fertilizer. Bees didn't care, but a person eating anything cooked with the honey could find themselves faced with a peculiarly sour aftertaste. Matt's honey was sweet and light, almost like corn syrup, with a complex earthiness like maple syrup baked in the sun. It was divine. Mina lost track of where she was for a moment, eyes closed, her tongue working its way up and down the spoon, finding every last drop of the sweetness.

When she opened her eyes, Matt was staring at her, an expression somewhere between ravenously horny and hypnotized by her hotness burning in his eyes. "Don't do that again," he warned.

"Do what?"

"Eat my honey."

"Is this a bear thing? Do your paws get stuck in the jar sometimes?"

"When you lick that spoon you are the sexiest thing I've ever seen and if you do it again I will take you right here on the floor but the floor is covered in blood and I don't want our first time to be like that. So please, no more spoon licking until I have all of this sorted."

Mina held up the spoon to her mouth and slowly stretched out her tongue. A deep growl rumbled out of Matt's throat and his eyes flashed golden for a moment. Maybe this wasn't the best time to tease him?

She filled a liquid cup measure with the honey and went back to her pie, tossing the apples in butter and honey until they were thoroughly and inextricably bound together. As Mina rolled out the chilled pie crust, men arrived. Wearing red jumpsuits and plastic face masks like a surgeon might wear, they went to work cleaning up the blood and bodies.

"Most of them escaped," Matt said to a stooped older man, half his size, with a heavy drooping white mustache.

"You got their leader. They'll never come back here again." He slapped Matt on the elbow, mostly because he couldn't reach his back. "You did good. Your dad would be proud."

"Thanks, Pop-pop."

The old man smiled at Mina from under his mustache. It was the same winning grin Matt employed so well. "Take care of him, will you? He's a good man but he needs a strong woman."

Mina nodded at the man, "Yes, sir."

The old man sniffed the air. "Oh, and save me some of that pie, would you? It smells divine."

"I wish I could," Mina told him. "But I plan to feed this whole pie to that wonderful man, naked, after he mates me." The heat flew into her cheeks and down into her belly. She'd meant it as a joke, but it wasn't. She was going to do everything to that big man that she could, then stuff him full of pie and do it all over again.

The old man laughed like a barking seal. "Oh you've lucked out here, Matthew. She's got spirit!" He winked at her again, then said in a whisper, "A word of advice, feed him a piece before the mating. It'll do wonders for his resolve." Pop-pop smiled benignly at the room, completely unfazed by his employees wrapping the bodies up in black plastic and hauling the away.

# # #

Pop-pop's cleaners were done before the pie was. They worked fast. The men usually cleaned the Lodge or the motels or the B&B. But Matt knew they did other jobs when the time called for it. He'd owe Pop-pop big for this one, that was sure. There'd be a price to pay, but not today.

When the last of the cleaners left, Matt surveyed the room. Apart from half his furniture being gone and one of the windows being completely gone, you couldn't even tell the room had been host to such violence. It felt like a home again, like a den.

The oven creaked open as Mina removed the pie and slid it onto the metal cooling rack Matt hadn't even known he'd owned. The smell of fresh baked apples, of flaky pie crust, of cinnamon and sugar and above all else, honey, grabbed him by the bear and shook him.

"If you eat a pie fresh from the oven, will it burn your tongue? Or is *forged by man*?" Mina asked with a wry smile. And then she caught his eyes. The bear was in charge now, Matt the man had fallen away. Sure he still looked like a man, walked like a man, but he was moving on instinct.

Mina slid the chef's knife from the block and sliced a generous piece of pie then used the flat of the knife to lever it seamlessly onto a plate.

"It'll be better once it cools. You should let it set before eating it."

The bear in him looked at her like she'd asked him to keep the sun from setting, like she'd asked him to juggle the moon. Then he scooped up the slice in one hand, mindless of the heat, and ate it in four slow, snuffling mouthfuls. When it was done, Matt fell back onto the floor with a thump.

"You've done it now, woman. My bear is thoroughly in love with you. He's always had a wicked sweet tooth, and that was the most delicious thing he's ever eaten.

You feed him that two more times, and he'll do whatever you ask."

Mina laughed then, and sat down on top of him, her strong thighs gripping his waist. She reached up and lifted her dress over her head then undid her bra, letting her flesh spill free. Matt watched her, transfixed. He never knew how so many men could put down curvy women when they looked so amazing naked. Mina stood for a moment, scooped a finger of hot apple pie out of the dish then smeared it thickly across her nipples.

"Oh no," she said, her voice breathy with mock alarm. "I seem to have spilled some pie on myself. I wonder who could help me clean it off?" Then, meeting his eye and grinning at him, she turned and ran giggling, up the stairs to the bedroom.

The bear and the man felt the thrill of the hunt in their blood. The taste of the apples and honey was thick on their tongue. And the scent of Mina's overpowering arousal swam in their heads. The chase was on. It was time. Matt let a rumbling growl ease out of his chest, shaking the walls and windows. From above, in the bedroom, he heard Mina squeal in surprise. In soft lopes, Matt crossed the living room, went up the stairs and burst into the bedroom, where he found Mina naked and stretched out languorously in his bed. She looked so small in the giant bed, so delicious.

"Someone's been sleeping in my bed." Matt's eyes burned with the need to mate. He could feel the bear in his bones, for once not resisting him. They both wanted this so bad. Mina had no idea what she was in for.

Mina's smile dazzled him. "Am I Goldilocks now? Are you going to eat my porridge, big boy?"

Matt crawled onto the bed next to her and buried his face in her pillowy breasts, he licked the pie from her in

A Slice of Honeybear Pie

long slow strokes, circling each budded nipple until he'd made sure every morsel of honey was gone. Then he switched to the other side. Mina whimpered under him, rolling her head on the sheets, pushing him away and pulling him closer.

"Oh yes, oh Matt. Oh fuck," she groaned as one of his hands slid down her soft belly to the wetness between her legs. He was a big man in every place that counted, he'd need to go slow with her but he wanted to throw her legs in the air and dive into her deeply, to spend himself immediately within her. The bear was impatient, but good for Mina, the man was not.

Matt curled his fingers inside her, stroking the slick tightness of her sex, rubbing his thumb against her clit while he held her nipple between his teeth and lapped at it softly.

"It's too much." Her voice was throaty, almost a growl. "Stop. Don't stop. Keep going. More, right there. Get away. No, Jesus, never stop doing that ever." The woman never stopped talking until Matt released her breast and kissed her. She cried out then, her legs bucking and squeezing against his wrist, as her climax overtook her. Matt kissed her as she came, their tongues dancing hesitantly then fiercer, learning each other's rhythms.

His cock hung heavy and hard between his legs, it's burning need to be inside growing more irresistible by the second.

# # #

Matt kissed his way down her body, nuzzling her neck, nipping at her nipples, circling her belly button with his tongue until she slapped his ears—it wasn't her fault, she was ticklish there—before spreading her thighs apart with those big strong hands of his and lapping at her cunt like a man on a mission to make her come so many times she'd forget her name.

Is this what being mated to a bear would mean? Sweet foods, generous sex, and a beautiful house in the woods? If so sign her up. She was ready.

The connection between them burned inside her. The heat had become an inferno, and every touch of Matt's tongue was just more fuel for her fire. He slid one finger and then two inside her, stroking her with powerful slow strokes, matching the rhythm of her breath until another wave of pleasure rose up and crashed into her, she screamed nonsense and clutched at his head trying to hold on, trying to shove him off, trying to never let his tongue get away.

It was amazing, but she wanted more. She wanted the real thing. Matt's eyes said he wanted—no, *needed*—it too.

Mina swung one leg over his head and rolled over onto her belly. It was by far her favorite position, though really they were all pretty good. Reaching past her soft belly she spread herself open for him. She glanced back over her shoulder and saw the giant, breathtakingly handsome man staring at her like she was the most beautiful woman in the world. Was this real or part of the magic of being his mate? Would it last forever? Would she be ninety years old and roll over in bed to see him gazing at her with the raw desire she saw churning in his eyes? Something told her she would. The connection they had felt like forever. It felt deeper than the ocean and stronger than the mountain under them.

The world come could at them, but it would break against their shores.

"What are you waiting for, big boy?" Mina purred. "Come over here and make me your mate."

After taking his time every step of the way, Matt's patience was clearly at an end. The man nearly leapt on top of her back in his hurry to be inside her.

"Easy," she cautioned. "Easy. Go slow, baby."

Mina watched his hands grip her hips, amazed at how perfect his tanned skin looked against her dusky hue. But then he nudged against her opening and her eyes snapped shut. She'd seen that he was hung like no man she'd ever seen, but the context had been lost on her. Matt was going to bury that giant cock inside her. If he had his way, he'd do it every day for the rest of their lives. Could she do that? Take all of him? She was about to find out.

With her hand, Mina stroked the thick tip of his cock and then guided it inside her. Matt hissed with pleasure at the sensation and a low strangled cry erupted from Mina's throat. He fit, just barely by god, but he fit. With one hand Mina clutched and clawed at the headboard, her trim nails peeling off flecks of paint. With her other hand, Mina rubbed her burning clit as Matt worked himself deeper and deeper into her, spreading her deliciously, impossibly open. It was as if he was made for her, made to touch every sweet spot at once, filling her completely. His cock was hard as steel and burning inside her. They were doing it raw, she realized. The idea of protection never even entering her mind. She'd never foregone a condom before—the sensations were so much more intense, so much hotter.

Matt nipped her shoulder with his teeth as he slowly moved inside her. He whispered into her ear then, the first thing he'd said in minutes, how he loved her. He told her she was beautiful. He told her she was wonderful. He told her how he'd never ever leave her. He whispered wonderful promises into her ear as he fucked her deep and hard, and he meant every one of them.

It wasn't long before Mina's orgasm ripped her apart, shattering her into a million beads of glass and throwing her to the wind. She cried out Matt's name as he eyes flew wide and gazed upon the brief infinity of her climax. And then Matt, too, was murmuring her name as he slammed hard into her and then with a roar emptying himself in a burning flood deep inside her womb.

"This is all happening so fast, but this and you and your house, it all feels like home to me. Like I've finally found a thing I didn't know I was missing all these years." Mina lay sprawled next to Matt, her body aching sweetly from their lovemaking.

"You could make a life here," Matt said. "The people in Bearfield are good people. There are no creepy shark men. I swear."

"This town is nice," Mina said. "But does Bearfield have a decent bakery? I saw those delivery trucks. All of these tourist lodgings, they could use some decent pastries."

Matt's belly rumbled. His bear must have liked the sound of that.

"I never really thought I'd find my mate," Matt said, his breath tickling the back of her neck. "I never thought I'd find you. It's rare, very rare, to find your true mate. Most of my people never find a true mate in all their years."

"Maybe if your brothers left your little secret village, they'd have better luck?"

Matt laughed. "Probably, but that's part of our paradox. We're solitary, but crave family and mates."

"Is that what I am? Your mate?" Mina wriggled against him, feeling the half-hard length of him twitch against her ass.

"I'd like you to be." He leaned over and kissed her neck, making her toes curl. "Would you like that?"

"What's involved? Do I become a bear, too?" She was exhausted, but the heat between them never dissipated, even after all they'd done she felt an insatiable need for him.

"Oh the usual," Matt said. "You don't become a shifter, but the claiming changes you. You'll be more than human. You'll need to be in order to care for the cubs."

Mina reached back and held his thickening cock in her hand, stroking it slowly. "Cubs," she said, her voice a purr. "I like the sound of that. Will we always feel like this? Or is this just a temporary heat between us? Will it go away once we mate?"

Matt guided himself into her gently, nudging her open. Mina gasped. Would she ever get used to his size? Did she want to?

"I've never had a mate before, but from what I've heard it gets even more intense when the mating urge takes hold."

Mina moaned as he thrust slowly into her, spreading her open again. "How could this possibly get more intense?"

"Let me show you," he said.

And then he did.

Recipe: Honeybear Pie

For the pie crust

Flour - 2 cups
Salt - 1 teaspoon
Butter - 1/2 cup
Apple Cider Vinegar - 2 tablespoons
Water - 6 tablespoons

To make two 9" crusts, combine the flour &
salt & butter in a food processor. Add the vinegar
and water and form into a ball. Wrap in plastic and
chill for 30 minutes.

For the pie filling

Apples - five cups, sliced thin
Honey - 3/4 cup
Cinnamon - 1 teaspoon
Flour - 1 teaspoon
Ground Cloves - 1/4 teaspoon
Nutmeg - a pinch
Vanilla - 1 teaspoon
Lemon Juice - 1 tablespoon

Preheat oven to 400°F.

Toss the apples in the lemon juice, then add the spices & vanilla & flour. Miss with the honey thoroughly and let sit while you roll out the pie crust.

Thoroughly grease your pie pan with butter or shortening, making sure to get the rim of the plate, and then gently fit your crust to the plate. Fill the bottom crust with the apple pie filling and then spend a few minutes licking the bowl and thinking about how amazing life is.

Fit the second pie crust over the whole pie, pinching the edges together gently. Cut slits in the top to vent the steam. My grandmother liked to carve hearts in her pie crusts or her favorite grandkid's initials, but feel free to do what you want. Though I'm told a J.S. cut into the top of the pie makes it taste all the sweeter.

You could be done now. Or you could take it to the next level of deliciousness, by rubbing heavy cream or melted vanilla ice cream into the upper crust and then sprinkling it lightly with sugar. It's not necessary, but it's what Mina would do.

Bake at 400°F for 10 minutes then **lower the heat** and bake another 40 minutes at 325°F.

Made in the USA
Columbia, SC
07 March 2021